Working Blue Press

First Edition

ISBN 978-1-967038-07-7 (Kindle)
ISBN 978-1-967038-08-4 (Print)

For all the women who love good sex,
and all the meals you've eaten while
talking about it with good friends.

Content

Suggestions for Further Reading

Girls Who Brunch Erotic Series
Books 1, 2, 3 and 4.

Follow Lacey Love on Amazon to keep abreast of new releases!

Seconds, Please

Girls Who Brunch Erotic Series

1

Seconds, Please

"Therapy works." Fawn plopped down into the flimsy chair of the quirky "cat" diner near one of several college campuses in Cleveland and smiled broadly at two of her brunch companions.

"Wow," Summer said with approval as she eyed Fawn carefully, taking in her new look. "You're practically glowing."

"Literally," Annie quipped. "That new platinum blonde bob is lighting up the patio. I absolutely love it—you look incredible."

"Damn right she does," Tabitha exclaimed as she rushed to the table, yanked out the neon green chair, and sat down with pride. "Did I do a fantastic job or what?"

Fawn chuckled at her enthusiastic friend, who had given her this new look over the weekend.

Tabitha was a hair and make-up genius, to be sure, and today she showed it yet again with her own look. She was sporting a white and silver mane that was tipped with hot pink to match her sparkling hot pink lips. Tabitha's plus-sized figure was curvaceously delicious in a turquoise slip dress accented perfectly by her silver, strappy heels.

The woman was full of color and pizazz, and she'd leant her special brand to Fawn's head in an adorable, platinum blonde bob that was an upgrade from her previous dishwater mane.

"So, what's the new look about?" Annie asked coyly. She leaned forward onto the wobbly glass table, her cranberry juice tilting in its glass. Her green eyes sparkled from under a Cleveland Indians ball cap as her long, golden locks touched her perfect breasts that filled out a matching tank top.

"Are you going to a baseball game with your hot men today?" Fawn deflected.

"Just Tommy," she said sweetly. "Christopher has to work."

"And how is throupledom?" Summer asked with an eyebrow raise as she took a sip of her prosecco.

"The sex is incredible," Annie laughed. "But the emotional part is…challenging, sometimes. As you might expect. How's sleeping with the boss?"

Summer's brown eyes sparkled as she laughed loudly and with an unencumbered joy. Her curvy, tight body, adorned in tiny, black shorts and a little gold crop top, shifted in her wobbly seat. "Ace is wonderful, thank you. No one at work is giving us shit, he's staying out of my career moves, per H.R., and the sex is the best I've ever had."

"Oh girl, that's my cue—tell us about the sex!" Tabitha squealed as the waitress hurried up to Fawn and Tabitha.

"Can I get you ladies a drink?" the young girl asked. Her bright blue hair lifted gently from the breeze.

"Mimosa for me today," Tabitha said. "Love the hair."

"Thanks," the spunky server replied.

"I'll take a whiskey sour," Fawn said smoothly.

"A wha—" Summer started. She was quickly interrupted by Annie, who asked, "Whiskey?"

"Did you say whiskey?" Tabitha finished off as they all stared blankly at her.

"Great, I'll be right back," the waitress said as she hurried off.

Fawn smiled to herself and then at the three pairs of questioning eyes staring back at her.

Fawn turned the conversation back to the black-haired beauty. "Is it love, Summer?"

Summer suddenly smiled with the same dopey sweetness that Fawn felt.

"It is," Summer said quietly.

"Oh my God, Summer," Tabitha said with sincerity. "Is it love, really?"

Summer grinned at Annie, who grinned at Fawn and Tabitha. *Annie already knows.*

"We said 'I love you,' last weekend." Summer shrugged with happiness.

"Oh, honey, yes!" Tabitha said excitedly. She reached across the table and grabbed Summer's hand with a shake. "Brunch on me!"

"I'm so happy for you," Fawn said. And she really was. Summer was a career girl and she'd never, ever given her heart away. But Fawn could tell, when they all met Ace at the Fourth of July barbecue, that he was different. "Are you happy?"

"Deliriously happy," Summer said. She leaned forward. "But today isn't about any of us."

They all turned to look at Fawn again and she could feel the blush rise from her neck to her cheeks. She smiled at its presence and knew it was time for her to spill the tea.

"Yeah," Annie said. "A few months ago, you suddenly had blonde highlights. And now you're a full-on platinum blonde—"

"Drinking whiskey—" Tabitha interrupted, as she was then interrupted by Summer who ended the questioning.

"And you're talking about how therapy works, and you've got a glow about you like someone in love."

They all looked questioningly at her.

"I am in love," Fawn said quietly.

"Is there someone else?" Annie asked earnestly.

"Are you leaving Stanny?" Summer added.

Fawn chuckled. "I promise you; I'm not leaving Stanny. *He* is who I'm in love with. My husband is who's making me glow."

"What the fuck?" Tabitha asked confused. "I thought I was dolling you up for divorce and dating again."

Annie and Summer eyed Fawn. "Well?" Annie asked.

"Explain yourself," Summer added.

"It definitely started with the idea I might want to leave Stanny," Fawn said as the waitress brought their drinks and sat them down.

"Ready to order?" she asked.

"Yes," Fawn said. "I'll take the all-you-can-eat pancakes. And I'll definitely be having seconds, please."

She smiled at the girls. "A phrase I've said a few times over the last couple months."

"Oh yes," Summer said. "I can get down with this new Fawn."

"Oh, I'm in," Annie agreed.

"Bitch, talk," Tabitha said excitedly. "You've been holding out on us."

Fawn smiled at the girls with a new attitude she felt all the way down to her bones. "It all started with Stanny's tie."

Fawn smiled as she started to talk.

2

Stale Stanny

Six months ago

Fawn hated lying to her friends about Stanny. They had asked her directly at brunch today why she looked so tired, and she had led them to believe it was because she'd been up all night sucking her husband's cock.

But really, she'd been up all night because of his snoring. She'd been pushing him to get one of those machines for his sleep apnea, but he refused.

"I don't need it," he had said tersely.

"You do need it," she'd yelled. "You know, you can die in your sleep from it without help. The machine just—"

"Fawn, stop," he had yelled back. His rich, dark eyes flashing with annoyance. "I don't need it. I don't want it. And that's the end of this conversation."

And then he had huffed off to work at his next construction site. He was a contractor and a damn good one. He was well-respected because he always kept his word and treated his customers with respect. He was like that with Fawn, too.

He treated Fawn like a goddess, and he had since the moment he said, "I love you," in the living room of her first apartment. They'd met in the complex when he was doing a construction gig building out the pool area. She had seen him working and thought his manicured beard and matching mustache were hot. So, at Tabitha's trusty advice,

Fawn had slipped on a bikini and offered him a lemonade.

"Thank you," he had said. He'd blushed as he'd guiltily taken in her petite frame and small breasts. "Appreciate it."

As his tall, thick frame had sipped the sweet and sour drink, she had asked when the pool would open, and one thing led to another. Within a year they were in love and engaged. He had never strayed, never looked at another woman, never treated her in a way that made her feel unsafe or uncomfortable. He was her man and he let her know that in the best ways possible, always.

"Fawn?"

"What?" Fawn looked up from the green screen set and smiled at the producer, Henry.

"You spaced out for a second," he laughed. He was dressed in simple blue jeans and a Sabrina

Carpenter T-shirt. "I asked if we're ready to bring talent on set."

"Oh, yes." She nodded as she tamped down the tape on the green screen paper and stood up. "You're good to go."

"Looks great." He glanced around at the set and nodded his approval. "You workin' on that action film coming to town next month?"

She nodded. "I am. I'm excited about it. A few big celebrities will be here."

"You ever wish you could do it in Hollywood?"

"I have done it in Hollywood," she quipped.

"Oh, that's right, I forgot," he said. "You were an assistant on that Oscar-nominated flick."

"I was," she said. "I was glad to come home, though."

"Stanny?" He grinned.

"Among other things."

"Henry! We need you for a sec," the director shouted.

"Catch up at the break?" he asked.

"Sounds good." Fawn nodded as he walked away. She waited until he was out of sight to head for the bathroom. She slipped into the corporate washroom with its black marble floors and stainless-steel faucets, then hid in one of the stalls. She needed to breathe for a second. *Why did I lie to my friends?*

She knew why. She was embarrassed. And also concerned. And also scared. She had thought about the "D" word, and she didn't want to admit that to them or anyone.

"I can't divorce Stanny," she whispered.

Well, she could. But she didn't want to. His parents had divorced when he was very young, and he'd never seen his father again. Her

parents had divorced and remarried
other people and she wished she'd
see them less. They were wonderful
and loving but a pain in her ass at
the moment.

"When are the grandkids
coming?" both of her parents
would ask.

"They'll come when they come
if we want them to," she always
said. And then she'd get the hell
out of there without another word.

Kids were something they both
wanted someday. Divorce was not.
Still, she couldn't get past the fact
that the sex wasn't as satisfying as
it was those first few blissful
months they were dating, before
they said "I love you" and got
engaged and she became Stanny's
wife.

The decline had been slow, but
she was certain it started right after
those three little words and went

downhill sharply after he put a ring on her finger.

She leaned back on the toilet in the bathroom stall as someone came in, checked their make-up, washed their hands, and left.

"Stanny, what's going on?" she had asked him during their first year of marriage.

"What do you mean?" He had responded, his dark eyes a sea of confusion. "We have sex all the time."

"Yeah, but," she had started.

"But what?"

"But…" she hadn't known how to say it in year one, so she let it drop. In year two, she got bolder.

"Can we just try something new?" she had asked.

"New, how?" he had asked. Gone was the confusion and in its place was vexation.

"I don't know, a new place, a new position," she had suggested.

"You're my wife, Fawn," he had said. "Not some whore off the street."

"I didn't ask you to treat me like a whore," she had said angrily. Nothing improved after that difficult conversation. And now it was year three and she was suddenly contemplating the "D" word.

She sighed as she pulled out her phone and scanned Instagram without really looking. Two women came in gossiping about the talent and how tired he looked.

"God, I hope make-up takes care of those bags under his eyes," the young girl exclaimed.

"No shit, right?" The other girl laughed. "God, I don't ever want to get that old. He's like thirty-five, Jesus."

The two laughed as they finished up and left.

Fawn was almost thirty and she didn't want to be thirty-five and not getting sex the way she wanted it from the one man who was supposed to be giving it to her. The man she loved and wanted to spend her life with.

But not like this.

Where had it gone wrong? The first time they had sex, he had bent her over her own kitchen table and slid that huge cock so deep inside her she swore to God she could feel that thing touch her stomach.

"Fuck me, Stanny, yes!"

"You like that?"

"Yes, God, yes," she had screamed. She had been so wet he slid easily in and out of her petite frame at a pace that made her come quickly.

"Fuck me again!" she'd yelled. And he had. He whipped her around, picked her up, slammed her against her wall, knocking the photos off, and pushed that cock inside of her.

"You like that huge cock in you?"

"Yes, Stanny, yes!"

"Look how huge it is in your tiny, sweet, little pussy."

And they both had watched him thrust in and out of her with joy.

"Slap my ass," she'd ordered.

He had carried her to the couch, dropped her on it, flipped her over, and smacked her ass so hard she thought she'd come right then and there.

"Like that baby?"

"More!" And he had proceeded to spank her as he drove that huge cock deep inside her.

"Come!" he had ordered. And she did, over and over.

The sex had been like that, wonderful and wild and with touches of light slapping and holding her down, until…

"I love you," she whispered to no one as she hid inside the bathroom stall.

And suddenly, it was like she had become fragile to him. The romance and gentleness were nice, of course. She wanted that kind of love, adored it and him, but the passion had virtually disappeared. It had become missionary most of the time, and vanilla. He treated her like a Queen.

And that was the problem.

We have to get that passion back.

She stood up and swung open the door with a ferociousness that caused it to bang against the other door to its left.

We are going to fuck like when we were dating if it kills me.

And he better get on board with it or else…she stopped the thought in its tracks.

*No, I'm not going there. I'm not
going straight to divorce.*
Not yet.

3

The Therapist

Stanny glanced nervously at Fawn, then back to the therapist, a strait-laced older woman with soft, brown hair and gentle eyes. She was a professional through and through and had been since they'd walked through her doors.

He wasn't comfortable here, even though the woman was trying to create an atmosphere that should make anyone feel at home. He recognized the design elements—water features for soothing sound, neutral tones for comfortability, plants and greenery for more oxygen and a relaxed feel. The materials were high-end, from the firm, comfortable couch they were seated on to the small, glass-front mini-fridge stocked with fresh fruit and water.

He was impressed. That quickly downgraded to impatience bordering on anger when she started talking Freud's Madonna-Whore Complex and how he might have it.

"I don't fucking have that problem," he bit back at her.

"Stanny—"

"I wanna fucking go, Fawn." He stood up and started to walk to the door, then stopped short of the handle and took a deep breath. He wanted to leave. He wanted to walk right out the fucking door and never look back.

Fawn.

He turned back to her. He had loved that woman since the first day he saw her. He knew she thought it started the day she brought him that lemonade in her little bikini. It wasn't.

He took a deep breath as he saw her eyes start to mist over at his anger. It absolutely killed him to see her cry. He walked back and sat down next to her.

"What were you thinking about just now, Stan?" the therapist asked.

"Nothing," he said gruffly.

"It was something," she said gently. "It made you turn around and come back."

Fawn leaned forward and grabbed a tissue. She wiped her eyes and blew her nose, then looked right at him. Her hazel stare could see into him in ways no woman ever had.

"I was thinking about the first time I saw Fawn," he said quietly.

"The bikini and lemonade."

"No," he said. "That wasn't it."

"What?" she asked. She peered at him in stunned silence.

He felt her eyes boring into him and he faced her with a smile.

"I saw you three days before that," he said. "You were with Tabitha. Actually, I didn't see you at all. I heard you."

"Really?" She grinned.

He nodded. "I heard you laughing. It made me feel…something."

He smiled as a blush erupted from her throat to her cheeks.

"I put my food down and peeked around the corner and then I saw you," he said quietly. "You had your hair in a bun and those Ohio State sweatpants I want you to burn."

She laughed and it made his gut fill with happiness.

"You had on a plain, white T-shirt and no make-up but…"

He glanced at her sheepishly.

"Your smile out-did all of it," he said. "Bright, happy."

"I knew I had to know who you were. I actually was going to ask you out right then, but my foreman called me back. And then…the lemonade."

"Stanny," she whispered.

"I don't wanna slap you, Fawn," he said. He shrugged. "I don't want to slap your body or tie you up, even if it is just sex. I don't want to do it."

"But you did it before, when we first started dating," she said.

"That was different."

"How? How was that any different?" she pushed.

"Because you weren't my wife," he said. "I love you. I don't want to hurt you."

He twisted his fingers and stared at them as Fawn shifted in her seat.

"Stan?" the therapist asked.

He looked at her with a sigh.

"What if what you're doing to her isn't hurting her?"

He shook his head in confusion.

"To Fawn, maybe it doesn't hurt," the therapist said. "Maybe it's pleasurable to have a light slap or a bit of bondage."

He frowned and glanced at Fawn. "Is that true?"

She tucked a dishwater blonde hair behind her ear. The blush on her cheeks was vibrant now as she nodded. "Just a little is all I'm asking."

He saw how difficult it was for her to say that. To admit to him that she liked something he hated. That she wanted something from him he couldn't give. *Or can I?*

He looked her over then turned back to the therapist. "I don't know how to do it without feeling the way I feel."

"What if you just start small?"

"What do you mean?" he asked. He glanced at Fawn and saw a hint of a smile. It made her happy to see him try. And all he wanted, ever, in this world, was to make her happy.

"I mean, start with something easy that doesn't hurt her."

"Like?"

"Like," the therapist said with a smile. "Start with your tie."

"My tie?"

"Your tie," the therapist said. She grinned as she closed her notebook and put it on the glass table. "Trust me, you'll know what to do with it."

~~~

Fawn smiled at her reflection in the large mirror of their top-of-the-line bathroom. Stanny had taken care with every single detail, from the beautiful white marble floor to the glass-door rainfall shower with benches and massage nozzles.
~~~

Nothing had been too good for her as he designed and built it.

She wanted to do the same for him now. The lingerie she wore was made from the silkiest material she could find. The cropped cream-colored top was just a little loose as it brushed against her hard nipples, making them stand out in the sexiest way imaginable. The thong fit snug against her skin and the strings in front cut across her hips in a flattering Bond-Girl type way.

She lifted his black tie from the sink and smiled at herself in the mirror.

"Here we go," she whispered.

She opened the bathroom door and clicked off the light. Immediately it was dark with flickering candlelight against the walls.

"Stanny," she whispered with delight. He had made their bedroom romantic with LED candles flickering everywhere and flower petals on the floor and bed.

He was standing by the bed in his black pajama pants. His hard cock pushed against the silky fabric.

"Fawn," he said softly. "Baby, come here."

He held out his hand and she walked slowly to him. *God, he's handsome.*

Stanny was a proud man and he carried himself that way. It was the main thing that had attracted her to him in the first place. He always stood with confidence, his six-foot, two-inch frame bold and unflinching.

Underneath that shield of armor was a thick, muscled body, cut from years of working in construction and playing football. He'd gotten a scholarship to play division three football and he graduated with a business degree.

He went to work construction after that and moved quickly through the ranks before opening his own contracting business two years ago.

She had fallen in love with him almost immediately and that only got deeper as time went on. Now, seeing him like this, trying something for her, to make her happy, she was falling in love with him all over again.

"Hi baby," she said sweetly. She slid her hands up his chest around his neck, the tie lingering near his nipples.

"You look sexy as fuck, baby," he said. He slid his big hands down her back and to her ass, gripping it as he kissed her deeply, then moving to her neck.

He kissed down her throat as his hands slid up under her little shirt and he pulled it off, taking her nipples, one by one, into his mouth.

"Yes," she moaned. She slid her
hands into his dark hair and guided
his mouth further south.

"Fuck, yes," he groaned. He
picked her up at the hips and laid
her on the bed, kissing down her
stomach to the top of her thong and
grabbing it with his teeth.

"Yes, baby," she said. His hands
grabbed the back of the thong and
his teeth held tight to the front. He
pulled them off her body and stood,
taking the panties out of his mouth
and holding them in his hand with a
smile.

She wasn't sure what he was
going to do next but the grin on his
face said she knew she'd like it.

He climbed on the bed and
straddled her as he grabbed her
arms and laid them behind her
head.

"Yes," she moaned lightly.

"You like that?"

"More." She could barely catch her breath as he took her panties and used them to tie her wrists together. "Yes, baby."

He slowly pulled the black tie out of her hands and dragged it down her body as he climbed off the bed and grabbed her ankles.

"Stanny, yes!" She could barely contain herself now as she felt her orgasm already building from just this simple act of him tying her up. "I'm so wet, baby."

He smiled at her, and she could tell he was trying to make her happy, and also not hurt her.

"Baby, you're not hurting me," she panted.

"You're okay?" he asked.

She nodded with a sexy smile as he took her ankles and lifted her legs in the air. He ran his thick hands from her ass, up the back of her thighs, all the way to her ankles, before taking them both in one hand.

"Fuck," she moaned. "Yes."

He took the tie and wrapped it around her ankles, pulling it into a soft knot. The pressure of the tie on her ankles and her panties on her wrists made her want to come. It was exhilarating to be under his control in such a vulnerable way.

"Tie it tighter," she said. When she saw him wince, she took it back. "Or not. Baby, it feels so good."

He smiled at her and tied it just a touch tighter.

"Yes," she moaned. "Fuck me, baby, please."

He smiled at her and slid his right hand down her leg, before sliding his thick fingers deep inside her, fucking her wildly with them.

"Baby! Oh God." She could feel her orgasm start to rise as he fucked her with his fingers harder and harder. Just when it started to crest, he stopped, dropped his pants, and shoved his huge cock inside of her, her tied legs over one thick shoulder.

"I'm gonna come!" As soon as that hard, thick cock slid into her tight pussy, her orgasm tumbled over the brink. "Keep fucking me, baby!"

She could see he was ready to come, too, her excitement driving him to the edge.

"Fawn, holy shit," he groaned. He slammed his cock inside her faster and faster, making a delicious smacking noise with his cock in her wetness. "I'm gonna come."

"I'm coming again," she yelled.

As he pumped her full of his salty release, she came hard and fast, her pussy spasming against that hard cock.

"Baby, yes!" The tension of the panties and tie made her orgasm even more intense. She loved it. She loved every second of it.

As they both started to relax, Stanny pulled out and quickly untied her ankles and wrists. He laid down next to her and kissed her gently.

"Are you okay?" he asked.

She rolled over onto her side to face him, kissing him gently. "Of course, baby. Are you okay?"

He let out a deep sigh. "I don't know, Fawn."

"You came, didn't you?"

"I did," he said.

"Come on, baby, admit it," she said gently. "It was a little fun."

When she got him to smile, she knew this might be the beginning of something fresh and fun for them both. And she appreciated his willingness to go there with her.

"I love you, baby," she said. "Thank you for this."

He nodded. He kissed her gently. "I did like the panties thing."

"There it is!" They laughed together as he let his guard down.

"Fawn, I don't want to do anything hard core," he said. "I just don't. I won't."

"Okay," she said. "Will you explore a little more, though?"

"How far?"

"Remember our first time?"

He nodded with a sexy grin.

She nodded back at him.

"Gotcha," he said. He trailed his fingers down her chest. "I can try and get back there."

"That's all I ask," she said.

They kissed gently and Fawn knew just what to try next.

4

I Don't Know About This

Fawn glanced at herself in the bedroom mirror of the plush hotel room she had rented and admired her new blonde highlights. They brightened up her face and made her feel more adventurous, which she hoped matched the new direction she and Stanny were headed.

As the knock at the door echoed through the room, she pulled on the chocolate brown wig Tabitha had lent her a year ago for a Halloween party. She pinned it quickly into place and ran her hands over the strappy black corset and thigh highs, no panties. Her pussy was freshly waxed and ready for Stanny's tongue.

She hurried past the bed in her black heels and eyed the handcuffs. They had pink fluff on them, and she hoped that their innocent appearance would make Stanny more receptive to their use.

She peered out the peephole and made sure it was her man, then she slowly opened the door with a smile.

"Hey baby."

"Holy fucking shit," Stanny said. His eyes looked like they were going to bug out of his head as he stepped into the room, shut the door, and wrapped those hands around her tiny waist.

"Yes, baby," she whimpered.

He dropped to his knees and slid his tongue between her pussy lips, slurping up her wetness with eager thrusts as she moaned as his beard brushed against her thighs.

"Fuck, Stanny, yes," she gripped his hair and spread her legs wider as he ate her with a ferocious need.

"God, woman," he said. He pulled back and stood up, ripping his shirt off and dropping his pants faster than a fireman. He ripped off his socks and shoes then picked her up at the hips and laid her on the bed. She saw him glance at the handcuffs before he tore the corset at the front letting her breasts pop out.

"Yes, Stanny, more!"

He dropped his head and sucked on her nipples at an achingly slow pace, licking one while thumbing the other, then trading.

"You're making my pussy so wet," she moaned.

"My cock is so hard, baby," he choked out. "You're so fucking sexy."

He sat up and smiled at her as he reached over and picked up the handcuffs. He held them in the air with a smile as she nodded.

He took one cuff and slipped it around her left wrist, cinching it.

"Get up," he ordered.

"Yes, baby," she said submissively.

As they stood, he pulled lightly on the wrist that was cuffed and led her into the bathroom.

"Straddle it."

She moved to the toilet and straddled it, facing the towel bar as he pushed his hard cock against her back. He slid his hands up her sides, then paused on her breasts, squeezing them and pulling her nipples as he took her mouth into a deep kiss.

"Fuck," she said as he released her. His hands slid down her arms, lifting them to the towel bar.

"Grip it." She did as she was told, and he slid the other handcuff behind the bar then latched the second cuff onto her right wrist.

"Yes, baby," she panted as she yanked on the cuffs, now secure to the bar. He dropped to his knees and ran his hands up her legs.

"Spread it wider."

"Yes, baby." She spread her legs and bent over slightly to push her pussy in his face. As soon as she did, she felt him thrust his tongue deep into her wetness as his hands grabbed her ass and squeezed. "Yes!"

His tongue moved up and down her slit as she moaned with pleasure.

"That feels so good, baby," she said. Just then, she felt a light slap on her ass. "More!"

He gave her another light slap on the cheek, and she wiggled with pleasure. "Fuck, baby, that's it."

She could feel her orgasm rising as he worked that pussy harder with his tongue.

"Fuck me, baby!"

He stood quickly and teased her entry with his thick tip.

"You like that, baby?"

"Fuck yes," she said as she pushed her hips against his manhood trying to pull him in.

"Oh yeah, you like that cock, don't you?"

"Fuck yes, baby." She groaned as he slowly slid it inside of her.

"You're so wet," he panted. "Fuck."

He gripped her hips and slid all the way in. He fucked her wildly as her handcuffs yanked on the towel bar.

"Holy shit, Stanny, yes!"

They both moaned with pleasure as he thrust harder and harder, every push and pull yanking on the towel bar more. Just as they both climaxed with one final thrust, the towel bar ripped out of the wall, hitting Fawn in the mouth with a bang.

"Ow," she yelped.

"Fuck," Stanny said with concern. He pulled out of her quickly and grabbed the bar, sliding her handcuffs off it. He dropped the bar to the floor, picked her up, and carried her to the bed. By then, she was in pain, bleeding, and laughing.

"Wow, Stanny," she said with a smile as she looked up at him. She immediately quit smiling when she saw his face.

"Where's the fucking key, Fawn?" He was panicked.

"Stanny, it's ok—"

"Fawn," he yelled. "Key."

"The table," she said quietly. She nodded to the little breakfast table as he rushed to it and grabbed the key. He came back even faster, undid the handcuffs, and threw them to the side. He raced to the bathroom and got a washcloth before wetting it under the sink with cold water. He came back quickly.

"Look at me." She did as he said, and he gently wiped the blood off her face. "I'm getting ice."

He pulled his pants on quickly and grabbed the ice bucket. He put a shoe in the door opening as he raced down the hallway.

"What the fuck," she whispered as she touched her mouth. She could feel her lip was swollen as she swallowed a little blood. She unpinned her wig and pulled it off as he came rushing back in with ice. He kicked the shoe out of the door as it clicked shut.

He rushed back to her and put ice inside the washcloth and wrapped it up as he held it to her lip. The look on his face was pain but also guilt. She reached up to touch him and he jerked away.

"I'm sorry," he said. "I'm so sorry. We shouldn't have—"

"Stanny, stop," she said. She pulled the ice away from her face. "You know it was an accident. What is going on with you? With all of this? This isn't just you not wanting to hurt me. This is something else."

He stood up and finished getting dressed. "This was a bad idea."

"No, it wasn't," she said. "This is me trying to get back to that passion we once had and you trying to avoid it. Why? Is there someone else?"

When he turned back to her, she immediately wished she hadn't said it. Stanny was a lot of things, but a cheater wasn't one of them.

"I'm sorry," she whispered.

"Let's go," he said quickly. "Please. Let's go home and take care of that."

She nodded as she stood and got dressed.

Whatever was going on with her husband, it went much deeper than just sex.

And things weren't going to improve until they talked through it.

5

No More Lies

Stan didn't want to lie to his wife. And technically he hadn't. He just hadn't completely told her the truth, either.

"Stan?"

He glanced up to see the therapist and his wife staring at him. Fawn looked so pretty with those blonde highlights. She didn't need them, but now that she had them, he noticed it made her face light up a bit. And he was all for that beautiful face having more light on it.

"I'm sorry, what was the question?"

"Why do you think you reacted as you did in the hotel room?" the therapist asked gently. She was wearing a cream-colored sweater today with black dress pants and simple heels. Her glasses were perched on her nose as her eyes bore down on him.

"It seems to me like you were actually enjoying yourself, and so was your wife," the therapist said. "It also seems like the towel bar was an accident. And yet, you treated it as though you did it on purpose. Why?"

His lips twitched. He wanted to tell Fawn. He truly did. She knew everything about him, except this. He meant to tell her when they first started dating and were talking about family. But then he decided against it when he looked in her hazel eyes. Then he wanted to tell her after they were engaged, but then it felt like he'd lied. And then he wanted to tell her after they were married, but he thought she'd feel trapped.

He glanced at his wife. He could swear the guilt was seeping from his pores.

"What?" she asked. Her face suddenly looked concerned. "You're scaring me, Stanny."

He saw a panic cross her eyes and he knew he had to come clean.

"I didn't exactly tell you the truth about why my parents got divorced," he said.

"What?" He could see confusion in her eyes. "What do you mean?"

"I would wake up in the middle of the night, I was maybe five years old," he said. "I'd hear my mom screaming. I'd run out and listen at the door. It sounded like they were rolling around. One time, she came out, and there was blood on her face."

"Oh my God, Stanny," Fawn said quictly. He glanced at her and saw her eyes fill with tears. It made his own eyes mist over.

"She said they were just playing. Everything was fine. So, I never asked again. I just stayed in my room when I heard it," he said. "I thought they were wrestling."

He shrugged as he felt his gut twist. He could feel tears brimming at the backs of his eyes, so he shook his head to clear them away. He cleared his throat.

"Go on, Stan," the therapist said.

He nodded. "Then one morning, I woke up and my uncle was there. My mom's brother. Randy."

He looked at the therapist, who nodded back.

"Why was he there, Stan?" she asked.

"He said my mom was in the hospital and my dad was gone."

He felt Fawn slide up beside him as she laid her head on his shoulder and wrapped her arms around him. He didn't want to cry, but he couldn't help the small burst of tears that jumped out anyway.

He fucking loved his wife. He didn't want to lose her. And if confronting his past was what it took to spend forever with her, this is what he was going to fucking do.

"Here," Fawn said quietly as she handed him a tissue.

He wiped his eyes as she leaned away to give him space.

"And then what happened?" the therapist asked.

"We went to live with my uncle while my mom recovered."

"Did you ever talk to anyone about it?" she asked.

He nodded. "My uncle took care of me. Took me to talk to someone."

His Uncle Randy had gotten him through those days. Helped him deal with the pain. Helped him stay on the right path. Took care of his mother until she got back on her feet. "I don't know where I'd be without him," Stan said.

"And how has it impacted your relationships?"

Stan shrugged. "I didn't ever really love anyone until Fawn."

He glanced at his wife, and they shared a loving stare. "I'm sorry I didn't tell you sooner."

She nodded.

"Why didn't you tell her sooner?" the therapist pressed.

"I thought she might leave me." He had never said those words out loud, but they were true and hit his gut hard. "I'm scared she'll leave me now."

"I'm not gonna leave you, Stanny," Fawn said quietly.

He nodded, then looked right at her. "I would never hurt you."

"Do you think you might or something?" Fawn asked.

He nodded and then he immediately shook his head. "I

mean, no, I would never. But when someone like that is your father, it just…it sits in the back of my mind."

He grunted a painful sound from his throat. "And you want to do this tying up and slapping and…what if it unleashes something and I can't stop or something? It freaks me out."

Jesus, he couldn't believe that came out of his mouth. He never thought he'd say those words to her, but here they were spilling all over the place. And what if she couldn't love him the same way anymore? What if she was scared of him? What if she didn't want to carry that through the gene pool with kids of their own?

"May I interject?" the therapist asked.

He tore his gaze away from his wife to his therapist, whose warm eyes gently stared at him. He nodded.

"Have you ever hit a woman, Stan?"

"No."

"Ever gotten so angry you couldn't control your words or actions with a woman?"

"No."

"Have you ever fantasized about hitting a woman or being violent with her?"

"Never."

"Have you ever thought about hitting Fawn or beating her?"

"Jesus, no," he spat. "Never. I would never hurt her."

"Stan, you're not your father," the therapist said. "And if you were ever going to be like him, you would have been him already."

"Oh," he said. He glanced at Fawn, who smiled at him.

"Stanny wouldn't ever do that to me," Fawn said. "It's not in him."

The therapist nodded with a smile. "Lucky for all of us, we have two parents. Which means we get genes from both sides. It seems to me like maybe you're a lot like your mother?"

Stan smiled at that comment. His mother was far from perfect, he knew that, but what she was, was endlessly kind and compassionate.

"I am, I think," he said. He nodded, then glanced at Fawn. "Do you think I'm like her?"

Fawn nodded. "Definitely."

She glanced at the therapist. "They're both really loving and funny and," Fawn paused for a moment. "When you're with them, you just feel…taken care of."

The therapist nodded with a smile.

"Excellent," she said. "Stan, let's start working on shifting your focus from fear of becoming your father, to love of who you are independent of him and even of your mother. Once we start to do that, I think what will naturally happen is that you'll start to loosen your grip on the fear of hurting Fawn, and you'll start to move toward a more satisfying sex life for both of you."

He nodded. "How do we start doing that?"

"Easy," she said. She closed her book and put it on the table. "You need to talk. And you need to be honest with each other. I'd suggest putting the sex aside in favor of a night in. Just spend some time getting to know one another all over again. You've both changed a lot since you got married. And you probably have future goals that you're looking to. Now is the time to be honest and talk through it."

They both nodded at her and then each other.

"And it'll fix this?" Stan asked.

"I can't tell you that," she said.
"All I can tell you is that honesty is
the foundation you need to build
everything else from. And it seems
like you both have struggled a little
bit with that. You need to talk
about why that it is. And how you
want to move forward in your
relationship with more honesty and
trust. And then we can go from
there."

Stan nodded, then peered at
Fawn. He smiled when he saw
nothing but love coming back at
him.

*I'll do whatever it takes to stay
together.*

6

Darkest Secrets

The ride home from the therapist had been solemn. Neither of them had spoken as Stanny pulled into the Chinese restaurant, then jumped out to grab their to-go order.

Fawn had taken that moment to inhale a deep, calming breath, and then breathe it out. What bothered her wasn't the truth—there wasn't a mean or dangerous bone in Stanny's body. He would never hurt her. That wasn't even the question.

The question was: Why did he lie about it? Or rather, why did he leave out the truth?

Doesn't he trust me?

She watched him jog out with the bag full of General Tso's

chicken, Shrimp Lo Mein, egg
rolls, and crab Rangoon's. The
smell hit her as soon as he opened
the door and she suddenly realized
that she was starving. She grabbed
the bag and put it on the floor
between her feet.

"Thanks," he said as he settled in
his seat.

"Of course," she said.

"We have wine at home?"

"Yeah."

They were quiet again as he
pulled out and headed toward their
quaint two-story in the suburbs.

"Why didn't you tell me?" she
asked. "It was a simple
conversation."

"It's not simple," he said. "Not
to me."

"You would never hurt me."

"How do you know?" he asked.
He stopped at a red light.

"Because Stanny, I've seen you
pissed off. I've seen you pissed off

at me. And I have never, in those moments, ever felt like you were going to snap and hit me. I would never have married you."

"What if that's what my mom thought, huh?" he asked. "What if she thought the same thing and then one day he just snapped. What if that's me?"

"Oh my God," she said. She shook her head. "Stanny, have you ever talked to your mom about this? About what happened?"

He gripped the steering wheel tighter and shook his head.

"Baby," she said quietly. "You're carrying a load on your shoulders you don't need to anymore. You need to talk to her. Because you and I can't really dig into this until you dig into that with her."

He was quiet as they pulled into their garage. He shut off the car. Neither of them moved.

"Fawn, what if she knew and married him anyway?"

Fawn took his hand and squeezed. "It was a different time then," she said quietly. "Women didn't have the same choices then that they do now. You can't judge her. You need to just talk to her."

She felt her heart squeeze as she saw his eyes mist over again.

"I'm scared to know the truth."

She nodded as he glanced at her. "Talk to her."

He nodded as she squeezed his hand again and assured him everything would be okay.

Because in her gut, she knew that it would be.

~~~

Stan sat with his head in his hands as he heard Fawn walk through the office door. He knew she'd heard him crying, and then
~~~

yelling again. Not at his mother, but at the way it had all played out. The conversation with his mom was over now, and they were in a better place, but going through it had taken more out of him than he expected.

"You okay?" she said quietly. She walked in and he moved his arms so she could sit on his lap. That's all he wanted. To lean into her body and hang on to her.

"I will be."

She sat down and wrapped her arms around his neck, pulling him close. "I love you, baby."

"I love you, too," he said quietly.

He gripped her tighter and inhaled her scent. A light musk with a touch of sweet vanilla.

"What'd she say?"

He took a deep breath and sighed. "She knew."

Fawn kissed his head then and pulled him closer.

"But you were right," he continued. "She didn't have many choices and she was pregnant."

"Pregnant?" Fawn sat up sharply. "What? I thought you weren't born until after they were married a couple years?"

"I wasn't," he said.

He glanced at her, then looked down again.

"Oh," she said. She looked at him questioningly.

"He beat her."

"Oh dear," she said quietly.

"She said when she got pregnant with me, she went to live with Randy until I was born."

"Oh, Stanny," she said.

He gave her a weak smile. "The good thing is my mom said I'm nothing like him."

"I told you that already," she said jokingly.

"Yeah," he said. "But it was good to hear it from her."

"Are you two gonna be okay?"
she asked.

"We are," he said. "We're gonna
be really good. We just needed to
talk about it. I needed to hear her
side and then be there for her. I
can't be mad at her or blame her.
She was a good mom. A really
good mom. She had it rough, you
know?"

Fawn nodded.

He sighed as he looked at her. "I
don't want us to end up like my
parents or your parents."

"I don't, either," she said. She
touched his face gently.

"When I married you, Fawn,
something clicked inside me that I
didn't want to ever touch you again
the way I had in the beginning," he
said. "I mean, don't get me wrong.
I loved it. It was fucking fun."

"Yeah, it was," she agreed.

"I just…I suddenly felt like there
was a new standard I wanted to

hold myself to," he said. "One that was completely different from…you know."

"I do," she said. "But we're not them. And Stanny, I love you. But I need that passion. I need it."

"I know," he said. He gripped her back. "Baby, I need it, too. I was holding myself back. I don't wanna do that anymore. I wanna be all in."

He couldn't put a price tag on seeing that grin light up her face. It was why he went to work every day and put money in a 401k and cleared the snow from her car and did all the things you do for someone you love for them to be secure.

"So, where should we start?" she asked. She wiggled her eyebrows.

"The bedroom," he said. "For a conversation."

"Oh geez, get me all excited." She laughed.

"Once we do that, then, we figure out the next part."

"I'd like that," she said.

"Me, too." He kissed her and knew they were going to be okay, so long as he could move past the emotional baggage that had caused this problem in the first place.

7

New Man

Fawn stepped into the shower and let the water work her muscles as she let out a deep sigh. It had been a month since Stanny talked to his mother and visited the therapist a few times on his own. And now, her and Stanny's relationship was noticeably different.

Once he got that thorn out of his side, he was a new man. He started to trust himself with her more and she started to be more honest with him about what she wanted.

She hadn't been doing that, she realized. She'd make a small attempt here or there and then drop it, but she wasn't being honest. Now, she was. She was trusting all her emotions, good and bad, with Stanny, and he was doing the same.

She smiled as the water massaged her body. It made her tingle in all the right places as she took the soap and rubbed her breasts with it. She stayed on her nipples and moaned a little as she squeezed them.

"Mind if I help you with that?"

She grinned.

"You're home early."

"Disappointed?" he asked as he stepped in with her.

She felt his hard cock against her back as his hands slid between her legs.

"Oh God," she moaned. His fingers slid into her wet pussy as his thumbs rubbed her clit. He stopped and she protested, but only for a moment as he slid his hands up her body, stopping on her breasts and squeezing them erotically.

"You like that, baby?"

"Fuck yes," she said.

He stopped and said, "How about this?"

When she felt the smack on her ass, she jumped. She turned and looked at him in surprise.

"Oh shit," he said quickly. "I'm sorry, was that too hard?"

"Sorry?" She laughed. "Fucking do that again."

His face transformed to raw pleasure as he slapped her ass again, harder.

"Stanny, yes!" She noticed he had a tie around his neck that he slowly pulled off. She smiled at him as he grabbed her and turned her around, pushing her against the shower wall.

"How does my cock feel against your ass?"

"So good, baby," she panted.

He slid his hands up her body and arms along with the tie. As he got to her wrists, he bound them in the silky fabric and held her arms against the shower wall.

"Fuck yes," she moaned. "Now, fuck me."

"Beg me."

"Fuck me, Stanny, please!"

She spread her legs as she felt him slide into her. When he did, he grabbed her wrists harder as he thrust deeper and deeper.

"Fuck yes, baby!" She pushed against his cock with her hips as he drove harder and harder into her. "Harder!"

He rocked deeper into her as he used one hand to hold her wrists and the other to slap her ass again.

"How's that baby?" he grunted.

"Again!"

He slapped her ass again as he slid skillfully in and out of her soaking wet pussy.

"I'm gonna come, baby," she yelled.

"I'm coming, too," he moaned.

She felt his grip tighten on her wrists as he filled her pussy with his come. "Fuck baby," he choked out.

"Don't stop," she moaned. "I'm coming."

As she came, he gave her one final slap on the cheek and her orgasm burst inside her like a water balloon, sending waves of pleasure over her body she hadn't felt since that first night he bent her over her table.

"Fuck, Stanny, yes." She squirmed her pussy all over his dick until she was certain she'd squeezed every bit of come out of his cock that she could. "Mmmm, baby."

"Fuck, woman," he said. "God you're amazing."

He untied her and helped her stand up straight as he turned her around and kissed her gently.

"That was amazing," he said.

"You liked it?"

"I loved it," he said. "Did you like it? Are you okay?"

She grinned. "Oh, baby, I loved it. It was exactly what I wanted."

"Me, too," he said.

He touched her face and smiled. "All I want is to make you happy."

"And I want to make you happy," she said.

"Oh yeah?" he asked.

She eyed him. "What? What do you want?"

"Well, there is something I want to try. Since we're being honest."

"What?" She wrapped her arms around him. "You've been holding out on me, Stanny. What is it you want?"

He grinned.

"Stanny!" She raised an eyebrow at him. "Your cock is too huge for my ass."

"Okay," he said. He smiled as he kissed her.

"But," she said. "You've done all this for me. I'll try for you, okay?"

"Really?" He smiled broadly.

"Really."

He glanced at her again.

"Are you kidding me?" she asked. "Now?"

"I mean, we can wait," he said.

She smiled at him.v"Get the lube."

"Holy shit!"

She laughed as he jumped out of the shower and yelled from the bedroom, "I've got it."

"I must love that man something fierce," she said as she shut the shower off and stepped out.

And she knew now, she really did.

.

8

What Happens Next?

No one at the brunch table said anything for a second as the waitress cleared their plates and dropped their checks on the wobbly top.

Summer finally broke the silence. "First of all," she said. "I feel terrible for Stanny about his dad."

"No shit," Annie said.

"What a fucking asshole his father was," Tabitha said. She chugged the last of her drink. "What do we all think Uncle Randy did to him? I think his dead body is somewhere in Lake Erie."

All the girls chuckled as Tabitha grinned. "I like Uncle Randy."

"You would," Fawn said with a laugh.

"Second of all," Summer continued as they all dropped their credit cards onto their bills. "I didn't realize all that was going on, Fawn. You could have talked to us about it."

"I appreciate that," she said. "I just…this sounds shitty, but it's not meant that way, none of you are married. It's different once you say those vows. I wasn't sure you'd understand."

"Well, we wouldn't understand the marriage part," Annie said. "You're right. But we would understand the fear of asking for what you want in bed. That's not an easy conversation to have."

"You're right," Fawn said. "I'm sorry. We just always came off as so happy, I wasn't sure how to tell you all it wasn't exactly as it seemed."

"We all have those moments," Annie said. "It's not all roses in my life. Throupledom is hard."

"Yeah, dating the boss isn't great all the time," Summer said. "Sometimes he's wrong about shit and then we fight or people see us and they say stuff. It's better, but it still happens."

They all looked at Tabitha. She shrugged. "What? I fucking love my life."

They all laughed as the waitress took their bills with their cards.

"But you're good now?" Annie asked.

"We're great now," Fawn said. "I mean, it's never perfect, you know, but it's perfect for us."

"I can't believe you were actually thinking about divorce," Summer said.

"I was miserable," Fawn said. "And I didn't know how to fix it. But, ultimately, I knew I loved him.

And divorce didn't seem right.
So…here we are."

"And therapy worked?" Annie asked.

"It was…a game changer," Fawn said.

"So," Tabitha said as the waitress dropped their checks with their cards. They all signed their bills. "What happens next?"

Fawn took a deep breath and sighed with a smile.

"We're trying."

"Trying for what?" Tabitha quipped as Summer and Annie teared up.

"Oh my God," Annie said as she smiled.

"Fawn," Summer said as she swatted at her eyes.

Tabltha glanced around the table and then suddenly at Fawn. "Fucking, no, bitch, a baby?"

Fawn laughed as Tabitha grabbed her into a hug, then let go.

"That little fucker is gonna love his Aunt Tabby. No, that sounds like a cat."

"Aunt Tabitha should do," Summer said. "Tabitha was a witch."

Tabitha grinned. "Much better. I fucking love it. Witchy, bitchy, Auntie Tabitha it is."

They all laughed as Fawn smiled.

"Cheers to the aunties," she said. They all clinked glasses as the morning turned to afternoon.

<u>More to Come!</u>

Fawn's love story isn't over! Keep reading the *Girls Who Brunch Erotic Series* to see what happens to Fawn and Stanny! Wanna learn more about the other ladies—Annie, Summer, and Tabitha? Keep reading the *Girls Who Brunch Erotic Series* as they have brunch, enjoy sex, and talk about it all!

Scan me

<u>Want to read more?</u>

Follow Author Lacey Love below
to get notifications every time a
new book is released. Want to learn
more about our other erotic series
Men Who Renovate? Then head to
workingbluepress.com!

Scan me

www.ingramcontent.com/pod-product-compliance
Lightning Source LLC
Chambersburg PA
CBHW031548310726
48971CB00008B/2671